PO THE CAT

A BOOK OF
MODERN-DAY FABLES

MOHANPAL SINGH DULAI

Po the Cat
Copyright © 2020 by Mohanpal Singh Dulai

All rights reserved. No part of this publication may be reproduced, distributed, or transmitted in any form or by any means, including photocopying, recording, or other electronic or mechanical methods, without the prior written permission of the author, except in the case of brief quotations embodied in critical reviews and certain other non-commercial uses permitted by copyright law.

Illustrated by
Greg Lawhun

Tellwell Talent
www.tellwell.ca

ISBN
978-0-2288-3594-3 (Hardcover)
978-0-2288-3592-9 (Paperback)
978-0-2288-3593-6 (eBook)

FOR BAYNTI KAUR

TABLE OF CONTENTS

Preface vii

Chapter I: The Story of a Stork 1

Chapter II: A Tale of Two Mice 13

Chapter III: Tick-Tock Clock 19

Chapter IV: Sitting Ducks 25

Chapter V: The Plight of the Turtle 35

Chapter VI: Straight from the Horse's Mouth 48

Chapter VII: A Catnap by the Fireplace 63

PREFACE

This book is intended for all of humankind. Much of life is mysterious, and to chronicle the events of a life in a meaningful way is a daunting task. I have, therefore, only narrated those tales from which the most insight and inspiration can be drawn. The ripples and echoes which emanated from these events are beyond imagination.

Mohanpal Singh Dulai

CHAPTER I

THE STORY OF A STORK

Once upon a winter night,
A stork prepared himself for flight.
Indeed, it was a silly sight,
For he was rather late.

His socks and boots he donned in haste.
He could afford no time to waste,
And in his rush, he ran and raced
To do what was his fate.

As you know, in this land and others,
Storks perform a great service to mothers,
Giving brothers to sisters and sisters to brothers,
Each night delivering babies.

But on this night this stork was tardy,
For earlier he had gone to a party
Where he ate a meal which was much too hearty
And had thought to himself, "Just maybe,

I should lie down and give myself rest
To allow the food that I ate to digest."
And with that thought he returned to his nest
And fell quite soundly asleep.

For hours on end, he slept, and he snored.
He dreamt of riches and lands of lore,
Of heroes and kings and storks of yore,
And his slumber was rather quite deep.

The minutes waxed, and the hours waned
As our hero the stork was rather sustained
In this unconscious state that kept him detained
When he suddenly burped and awoke.

A moment it took for him to assess
Who and where he was, I confess,
When he said to himself, "I still have to dress
And make my deliveries to folk!"

His baskets were due on their porch steps by dawn,
So he grabbed the map where his route was drawn.
He stretched his legs and let out a yawn
And thought that he might now be fired.

It was dark, but the coming of day grew near.
So he gathered his goggles and garments and gear,
For now the stork was in frightful fear
Of never again being hired.

He tightened his boots, and a scarf he wrapped.
To warm up his wings, he fluttered and flapped.
Again, he regretted to have napped
And took off in flight to the moon.

PO THE CAT

It's a well-known fact that the moon's full of pocks,
Riddled with ridges and ranges and rocks.
The terrain's not conducive to leisurely walks
And won't be any time soon.

But it's a little-known fact that on the dark side
Of the moon is where all the babies reside,
Laughing and frolicking side by side
'Til a stork comes and brings them to Earth.

And so with the cold biting his face,
The stork flew until he had reached outer space
And landed on the moon with such delicate grace
That it brought all the babies such mirth.

But our fine-feathered friend was clumsy indeed,
And to his assignments he hadn't paid heed.
And now he knew not which baskets he'd need,
So he grabbed the first three in sight.

Three baskets in beak, the stork flew away,
Inside, three blanketed bundles lay,
Racing against the coming of day
And the going away of night.

He flew to Earth to make his rounds.
At tremendous speeds he covered the grounds
And delivered the first two just as the sounds
Of morning began to be heard.

As the light began to invade the land,
The snow shone bright like crystal sand.
The end of the task was near at hand
As the stork delivered the third.

To a house on a farm this third baby went,
And for caring parents this baby was meant.
But our friend the stork was tired and spent,
And his error the stork never saw.

For when he laid the basket by the door,
He rang the bell and turned to soar.
But if he had turned and looked once more,
He would have seen the paw.

PO THE CAT

It protruded above the basket's rim,
Too furry and small for a human limb,
The color of gray and rather slim
With claws that could tear through meat.

But the stork was already flying away
When the door to the house opened up to display,
To the woman who stood there, the basket which lay
On the porch right in front of her feet.

Though expecting a child, she was suddenly smitten
By a most adorable solid gray kitten.
So let it be noted, and let it be written
That she took the cat into her home.

PO THE CAT

A kitty whose nature was calm and polite,
In connecting with others he took great delight,
And he cherished the farm, a remarkable site
    With plenty of places to roam.

He knew not then what his future would hold,
That as he grew old, he'd become wise and bold,
And of his wisdom great tales would be told
    With reverence wherever he sat.

But that night he slept by the fireplace flame,
His mind forging fictional fortune and fame
That someday, perhaps, would be his to claim,
    And his name became Po the cat.

CHAPTER II

A TALE OF TWO MICE

Together they sat on the kitchen floor,
    Two mice, hungry and keen.

For them finding food was a challenging chore,
    For this house was spotlessly clean.

But now they stared at a piece of cheese
    Which rested upon a trap.

Said mouse one, "Dear pal, if you please,
    I am indeed a brave chap.

I shall get that morsel, my rodent friend,
    Despite that deadly device."

Mouse two exclaimed, "You should comprehend,
I fear it will be your demise!

Many a rodent have thought like you,
Most of whom ended up dead.

Those who survived are extremely few,
So dismiss the thought from your head."

The first mouse replied in a heady tone,
"I will have that cheese to no end!"

Said mouse two, "Then you go alone,
But please be careful my friend."

So venture forth did he, mouse one,
To claim this ultimate prize.

With a hop and a jump and a skip and a run,
He approached with ravenous eyes.

Such a piece of cheese he had never seen.
The smell was quite overcoming.

"I will quickly grab it since I am so keen
And return to my nest in the plumbing."

Such were his thoughts as he sized up the trap
And prepared to gamble with death.

Then all of a sudden, his tail made a snap,
And the cheese rolled off to the left.

Mouse one quickly jumped out of the way,
The trap missing him by a hair.

He thought, "I am truly lucky today,"
For it gave him a sizeable scare.

A little shaken and overly proud,
Mouse one turned and looked at mouse two.

"I told you I'd do it!" He yelled aloud.
The other replied, "Good for you!

PO THE CAT

Now, my dear friend, please do hurry back
And share your prize with me."

"I'll do no such thing because of your lack
Of faith, so wait there and see.

I shall eat this cheese and share none with you."
Asked the second, "Not even a bite?"

Replied the first, "No, until you do
What I have done here tonight."

With a sheepish grin, mouse two replied,
"But I lack the nerve for such toils."

Mouse one shot back with a pompous pride,
"Then alone I shall feast on my spoils!"

As he prepared himself to savor the taste
And enjoy it with all of his soul,

The young housecat pounced on the rodent in haste
And swallowed the first mouse whole.

MOHANPAL SINGH DULAI

CHAPTER III

TICK-TOCK CLOCK

Tick-tock, tick-tock,
The ticking of the marvelous clock,
How it ticks and tocks to no end.

Onward traveled Father Time,
And Po the cat, now in his prime,
Wished to have a word with a dear friend.

"See here," said Po to the fish,
"Watch the pendulum swoosh and swish.
Watch the clock with ever-moving hands."

Said the fish, "I do not care
Whether the hands are here or there.
The time of day does not affect my plans."

PO THE CAT

Tick-tock, tick-tock,
The ticking of the steady clock,
The sands of time will never cease to flow.

"But surely you will mind the time.
Ignoring it would be a crime.
How else to stay on schedule?" inquired Po.

Replied the fish, "It matters little.
When I am hungry, I'll eat my vittle.
When I am sleepy, I'll close my eyes to rest.

But if not tired, I'll not sit still.
The sun and moon set where they will,
On them I don't rely to be my best."

Tick-tock, tick-tock,
The ticking of the rousing clock,
Forever bright burns the candle's flame.

Po exclaimed, "But don't you care
Whether or not there's time to spare
To work and learn and fulfill your life's aim?"

The fish shot back, "I have no work,
No chores, no tasks, and that's the perk
Of being a fish with never a worldly care.

I swim and play and frolic all day,
Do what I want and say what I may.
Enjoying the moment is all I will ever dare."

Tick-tock, tick-tock,
The ticking of the daunting clock,
The old man's beard grows mighty long and gray.

Po's frustration grew and grew.
"One can't sit idly by and do
Nothing productive and waste away one's day!

We are here, but our time is short.
And soon our ship will leave the port.
So don't waste time. Make worth of your short life."

"It is not a waste," said the fish,
"To be myself and do what I wish.
And for it I haven't the slightest bit of strife."

Tick-tock, tick-tock,

The ticking of the precious clock,

The world, it seems, will never cease to turn.

The clock stared Po in the face.

His feline heart began to race.

Frustration swelled, and his anger began to burn.

The fish smiled back without a care,

Swam to and fro with a casual air.

And Po, to himself, suddenly admits

That while they argued back and forth,

His entire day of such cherished worth

Was wasted in a worthless war of wits.

Tick-tock, tick-tock,

The ticking of the marvelous clock…

CHAPTER IV

SITTING DUCKS

As time went by,
Po would try
To go on a daily stroll.

He'd contemplate things,
Whatever life brings,
Searching deep within his soul.

One day he was out,
And while walking about,
He happened upon a pond.

PO THE CAT

Some voices he heard,

His curiosity stirred,

So he crouched to hear the voices beyond.

He saw from his stoop

Four ducks in a group.

In the clear blue pond they were sitting.

A fifth duck was standing

While the others demanding

That her behavior was unbefitting.

Said the four to the one,

"Well if you are done

Standing, then please come and sit."

Said the one duck,

"It is just my luck

That I'd like to stand for a bit."

PO THE CAT

In a pompous tone,

The other four groaned,

"Please sit and cease to stand."

The one duck said,

"Well it is in my head

To continue on as I'd planned."

The other four replied,

"Well you may be denied

Acceptance if you do."

The lonesome said back,

"I am under attack

For being different from you!"

The other four birds

In unison towards

The standing duck together stated,

"You are an odd duck,
And now you are stuck
With forever being alienated."

Now, Po the cat
Wouldn't put up with that
And decided he should interject.

So he walked by the group,
And he looked at the troupe
But addressed the duck standing erect,

"Nice day to stand tall
With confidence and all,
Up on your own two feet."

With those few words,
Po left the birds
And continued to stroll down the street.

PO THE CAT

Each duck faced the others,

Reconsidered their druthers,

And suddenly altered their views.

"You know, sitting is boring,

And don't be ignoring

That sitting too long gives you the blues.

Yes, standing is good

As every duck should

Get blood flowing into the legs.

We hear it is best

To avoid too much rest,

Which will help you lay better eggs."

So the four sitting ducks,

With some quacks and some clucks,

Stood up to be like the one standing.

PO THE CAT

The one looked at the four,

Who now seemed even more

Deserving of some reprimanding.

But thinking it through,

She knew what to do.

And without a smile or frown,

She looked at the four,

Who harassed her no more,

And the odd duck gently sat down.

CHAPTER V

THE PLIGHT OF THE TURTLE

In the morning sun, devoid of fog,
An old turtle sat upon a log
When a small and furry chipmunk approached with glee.

"Hello, Mr. Turtle! What a good day!"
"A bunch of nonsense is what I say,"
Said the turtle, "The day's not good to me.

You see, little beast, my blood is cold.
Well that, at least, is what I am told,
And I must always warm myself in the sun.

How lucky you are, warm-blooded are you.
So you see, you are ignorant and haven't a clue
'Cause sitting here all of the day is really no fun!"

The chipmunk, in a state of fright,
Scurried away and out of sight,
Leaving the turtle all alone once more.

The turtle grunted and shifted a bit
And said to himself, "What a nitwit!"
And continued with his sunbathing as before.

Down the trail a rabbit hopped.
In front of the turtle, the rabbit stopped
And greeted him with a low and courteous bow.

"How are you, my dear old pal?
Tell me please, if you shall,
What do you do to stay in shape and how?"

"I find your words and tone sarcastic,"
Said the turtle, "and quite bombastic!"
The rabbit replied, "I did not mean to offend."

"Well instead of rubbing it in my face,
Please just leave and give me space
And accept that a creature like you cannot comprehend."

The turtle continued, "I am weak.
I'm terribly slow, and my joints all creak.
I wasn't endowed with the vigor with which you were."

Finding the turtle's response absurd,
The rabbit left without a word,
Quite displeased with what he had to endure.

As the turtle savored his crochety mood,
An ant emerged in search of food
And looked up at the turtle and said, "Hello.

I'm hungry and looking for some direction.
Food is scarce, and upon reflection,
I thought I'd look above ground instead of below."

The turtle rolled his eyes and spat,
"You poor insect, so nice and fat,
You're right to say that food is scarce, it's true.

But your colony won't let you starve to death,
While I dine alone. So with your next breath,
Leave my sight before I decide to eat you."

Startled and shocked beyond belief,
The ant ran for cover under a leaf,
And the turtle let out a sigh in shear disgust.

All of these creatures, so rotten and spoiled,
Had no idea how hard he had toiled.
He'd always worked hard and often been left in the dust.

He closed his eyes and reviewed in his mind
All fusses and frets he could feasibly find
And felt furious, forlorn and frustrated with his plight.

After a while he opened his eyes,
And standing before him, to his surprise,
Was quite an unusual and unexpected sight.

An old gray cat with a furrowed brow,
And as much disapproval as his face would allow,
Opened his mouth and slowly started to speak.

"I've watched you now for quite a while.
You never say thank you, and you don't smile.
But please don't take offense at my critique."

PO THE CAT

The turtle listened, remaining leery.
The cat continued, "Your outlook is dreary.
But can't you see that life is wondrously grand?"

The turtle shot back, "It's tough for turtles.
Nature is cruel, and life's full of hurdles.
So you see, us turtles have all been dealt a bad hand."

"The glass is half-full," Was the cat's retort.
"Take the chipmunk, whose life is so short,
While you will live a lengthy life, indeed!"

The turtle admitted the cat's point was true.
He'd done much in his life, with much yet to do.
That a long life was good, this point he had to concede.

"Remember the rabbit?" The cat went on,
"Despite his agility, speed and brawn,
You beat him because slow and steady wins the race."

PO THE CAT

The turtle thought back to the glorious way
That he'd won the race and seized the day
And agreed that even a turtle can be an ace.

The cat continued on with his lecture,
"Consider the ant and his architecture.
His home falls apart whenever a gusty wind blows.

Many times a day the ants must scurry
To rebuild their hill in a rush and a hurry,
While you don't suffer their fate, as everyone knows.

Your house you carry on your back,
Protecting you from harm and attack,
Keeping you warm and safe wherever you lie."

The turtle considered the words being said.
Without his shell he'd probably be dead.
It really did come in handy, he couldn't deny.

So he began to view in a different light
All of the things of which he'd lost sight
And realized that the cat was right and sincere.

The turtle then reinvented his life,
Taking his bad luck, hardship and strife
And turning it into hope, well-wishes and cheer.

He soon became known for his upbeat view.
It's ironic and strange, but yes, it's true
That others began coming to him for advice.

And thus the turtle lived out his days,
Imparting to others in numerous ways
That a rotten outlook on life just won't suffice!

CHAPTER VI

STRAIGHT FROM THE HORSE'S MOUTH

On a farm and in a barn,
In a stall stood a big white horse.
Concerned with the comings and goings of others,
Of gossip he was often the source.

So when Po showed up, the horse curiously said,
"Hey there! Doin' alright?"
"Oh, I am fine," replied Po the cat,
"But ever since late last night,

In the back of my throat, just behind my tongue,
I've had an annoying tickle."
Said the horse, "I hope you can figure out something
To help you out of this pickle."

With a thanks and a wave, the cat moved along
And left the barn through the back.
But upon his exit Po was seized
By a violent coughing attack.

He hacked and coughed as his eyes turned red
And his face turned a bright shade of blue,
Until up from his stomach and out of his mouth
Came a furball the size of a shoe.

Po stared at this big matted ball of fur
Now laying upon the ground,
And he felt much better as the cause of his ailment,
He realized, had just been found.

But he thought to himself, "I should rest," as the
Wheezing and coughing had rendered him weak.
So by the fireplace Po slept deeply,
Rejuvenating his physique.

Meanwhile, the horse decided to tell
The bull how Po looked weary.
"He didn't look well, his stride was all off,
And he looked rather tired and dreary."

Said the bull, "Oh my! I hope the old fella
Has not gone and caught a bug."
The horse said, "He almost certainly has,"
And turned around with a shrug.

A worry wart in every respect,
The bull was now very concerned.
He thought he should let the chickens in
On everything he had just learned.

PO THE CAT

"Po the cat is sick.
Alas, my friend, he is not well!"
Replied the hens, "Please say more,
Now you really must tell."

Said the bull, "It seems he has caught a virus,
In that there is little doubt."
"Are you sure?" asked the hens. "Well you see,
I heard it straight from the horse's mouth."

As is their nature and temperament,
This bunch of cackling hens
Decided to go their separate ways
To inform every one of their friends.

The pigs began to sob and moan
While rolling around in the mud.
The cows were taken by such surprise
That they choked upon their cud.

To a group of goats and a gaggle of geese
Is where the story next spread.
The rabbits thumped when they heard
That Po was just holding on by a thread.

As the news meandered across the farm,
The story festered and grew.
It gained new features and facets and facts,
Adding new elements to the stew.

From whence it came and to whom it was told,
It really cannot be said.
But the rumor arose from amongst the chaos
That Po the cat was dead.

Paranoia emerged from amongst the beasts,
And panic began to set in.
The creatures all succumbed to the fear
Which arose deep from within.

The donkey amidst his hee-hawing
Proceeded to eulogize,
And the owl exclaimed, "We mustn't remain!
To stay here would be unwise!"

They feared the virus would get them, too,
So the sheep ran away up the hill.
The peacock plucked a colorful feather
And started writing his will.

The fowl and fish and frogs all fled
To the far side of the pond.
The groundhogs all abandoned their burrows,
Of which they were quite fond.

"His face was green, his lips were blue,
And pus oozed from his ears."
The pigs, upon hearing this news,
Again were reduced to tears.

All of the creatures prepared themselves
To flee to a safer land,
Except for the ostrich, who couldn't be swayed
And just stuck her head in the sand.

But she asked the jays, "Who told you that
It'd be safer to fly away south?"
A fledgling replied, "We practically heard it
Straight from the horse's mouth."

They all thought a virus would ruin the farm
And all that resided therein.
So they packed their things and prepared for the
Evacuation to begin.

PO THE CAT

Inside the house, Po awoke
Feeling rested, alive and well.
But he heard the hoopla and wondered
What could cause such noise to swell.

Amidst the screeches and cries and howls
Over Po the cat being dead,
The wise sage emerged from the farmhouse
And stood there scratching his head.

Suddenly, the farm became very still,
And all of the creatures were quiet.
So Po asked, "To what do we owe
This loud and obnoxious riot?"

Nobody spoke. They all just stared,
Unable to comprehend.
None could believe that standing before them,
Alive and well, was their friend.

After a pause, the bull spoke up,
"At first we heard you were ill.
And then we all heard that your breath had ceased
And your heart had become cold and still."

Po stared. "What nonsense!" he said,
"From where could such stories be born?"
But all were silent, and none would speak
As they now feared Po's scorn.

"Tell me, my friends, who convinced you
That I was no longer alive?
As you can see, I live and breathe
And shall continue to thrive."

The owl explained, "When we heard you were sick,
Our imaginations ran wild.
The culprit, we heard, was a virus that would
Infect every grownup and child."

"Is there fact behind this fabulous fable?
 Did nobody ask for proof?"
Po inquired, "Did anyone bother
 To question this outrageous spoof?

I'll give you advice and impart some wisdom,
 So everyone please gather near."
On he continued, "For goodness' sake,
 Don't believe all that you hear.

Who started this rumor? Who told this tale?
 Which one of you spread it about?"
Then the creatures all cried in unison,
 "We heard it straight from the horse's mouth!"

CHAPTER VII

A CATNAP BY THE FIREPLACE

An aged Po curled up on the floor
In the warmth of the fireplace flame,

When he heard a voice ask from within his core,
"What has been your life's aim?"

He considered how great his life had been,
So full of riches galore.

He had not a want or a wish from within.
He could not have asked for more.

PO THE CAT

Many lives had molded the shape of his path,
Unpredictable, winding and malleable.

But the journey had yielded an aftermath
Of treasures he knew were invaluable.

He had heard of the stork who had carried him here
As a newborn bundle of fur.

What chance! What fate! Life's methods are queer!
Thoughts of happenstance conjured a purr.

His youth had been nurtured by guidance and love,
which had shaped his outlook and attitude.

At night when he'd stare at the stars up above,
He was filled with a great sense of gratitude.

He fondly recalled each and every friend
Who had taken his counsel to heart.

To them many thanks he had to extend,
For they all had played their part.

They were the ones who had taught him so much,
And *he* was the one who had learned.

He had listened, observed, and as such,
Their confidence Po had earned.

He'd touched many lives, and in turn, they his,
A higher understanding achieved.

Eliminating hatred and prejudice
Was a purpose in which he believed.

To be humble, perchance one of life's greatest lessons,
Yet, realize one's own self-worth

Had become one of Po's greatest obsessions,
Something he'd strived for since birth.

But still the question remained in his head,
"What has been your life's aim?"

Looking upon the path he had tread,
Apparent the answer became.

"I accept, without doubt, all which comes to be.
Yet, I forge my own path beyond.

PO THE CAT

I may not dictate what happens to me,
But I do control how I respond.

My aim has no beginning or end,
Not a tangible thing to be held.

To align with my nature, as I comprehend,
Is something to which I'm compelled.

So I aim to accept all that's been done
And embrace who I am down deep."

Thus, knowing that he and the cosmos were One,
Po the cat fell asleep.

THE END

www.ingramcontent.com/pod-product-compliance
Lightning Source LLC
LaVergne TN
LVHW011855060526
838200LV00054B/4350